John Samuel Robinson is a storyteller, something he inherited from his Irish heritage, and has written across all genres, including song, poetry, and stories. He and his wife, Karin, have two children, Sean and Claire, and a granddaughter, Eleah. John's career has been rich with many colourful experiences, working for an international airline and in the newsroom of a Sunday newspaper publication. Now, in semi-retirement, he's left the best for last with his imagination and new publication, Knocknagree. John lives in Auckland and is a member of the New Zealand Society of Authors.

John Samuel Robinson

KNOCKNAGREE

AUSTIN MACAULEY PUBLISHERS
LONDON · CAMBRIDGE · NEW YORK · SHARJAH

Copyright © John Samuel Robinson 2025

The right of John Samuel Robinson to be identified as the author of this work has been asserted by the author in accordance with sections 77 and 78 of the Copyright, Designs and Patents Act 1988.

All rights reserved. No part of this publication may be reproduced, stored in a retrieval system, or transmitted in any form or by any means, electronic, mechanical, photocopying, recording, or otherwise, without the prior permission of the publishers.

Any person who commits any unauthorised act in relation to this publication may be liable to criminal prosecution and civil claims for damages.

This is a work of fiction. Names, characters, businesses, places, events, locales, and incidents are either the products of the author's imagination or used in a fictitious manner. Any resemblance to actual persons, living or dead, or actual events is purely coincidental.

A CIP catalogue record for this title is available from the British Library.

ISBN 9781035884438 (Paperback)
ISBN 9781035884445 (Hardback)
ISBN 9781035884452 (ePub e-book)

www.austinmacauley.com

First Published 2025
Austin Macauley Publishers Ltd®
1 Canada Square
Canary Wharf
London
E14 5AA

I wish to thank our widowed grandmother, Granny Robinson, who courageously left her Dublin home in 1921, to settle on the other side of the world in New Zealand with her six children. One of the six was my father, Jack Francis Robinson, whom I would also like to thank for his story telling at mealtimes around the kitchen table and his love and dedication as a loving father and family man. I am proud of my Irish heritage. Thank you also to my late mother, Margaret Ora Robinson, for her encouragement to write and my dearly beloved twin now deceased, Mary. Thank you also to my sister, Frances O'Hanlon, for her support and whose sharp eye for detail contributed with proofreading and a great big thank you also to Sunny Sawhney.

Chapter One

"Your last caller Mikey must be dreaming; time travel is impossible – you would need a time machine as big and as powerful as a complete universe before considering time travel."

"He's not in the real world. Wake up Mikey, it's all in your head – knock, knock, is anyone there?"

Mickey grinned and nodded in agreement towards his radio, blearing out from the back room.

"He's right," Mikey thought, "Yes, it is all in my head."

Talk-back radio is good entertainment for Mikey and helps keep him amused and well-entertained throughout his long retirement days.

"It is like having a room full of guests all chirping away," he mused muttering away to himself.

He was well away from the politics, backstabbing, and toxic working environments, now he can listen to others calling in to bleat and grizzle.

He's now mortgage-free snug and secure in his own home, feeling connected again but this time without any worry, guilt and stress.

Now, there is never an idle or boring time for Mikey. He can do as he pleases, see, and speak to whomever he chooses and organise his own time even when to eat, shit and piss using his own bathroom without the uncomfortable feeling of knowing others were also sharing and sometimes listening in an adjoining cubicle.

Mikey still has a healthy network of close friends and working colleagues with whom he also keeps in regular contact.

Mikey has plenty to talk about and discuss on radio talkback and has developed his own following amongst listeners, being also a regular caller and contributor to shows.

Mickey is popular with a soothing romantic voice that late-night callers like to listen to and often compliment him suggesting that he should also become a host.

He feels a sense of privilege that he's able to piggyback his own popularity off Bill Markham and is pleased with himself that he has developed his own set of groupies.

Mickey, however, loves his privacy too much to entertain, ever becoming a public figure.

He nevertheless enjoys his elusiveness and appreciates that he has become his own enigma.

He is a speed freak and loves fast cars.

He reads and has a collection of Popular Mechanics magazines and is fascinated with time travel.

He believes in parallel worlds and multiverses and that we all have a doppelganger, despite never coming across one yet.

He did once see his Guardian Angel, well at least that's what he believes it was.

While passing the bathroom door, he was startled to notice a shadow high upon the wall.

When he turned to take a second glance this shadowy being almost translucent, stared back mysteriously at him with a wry expression.

As he opened his mouth to speak, it disappeared.

The experience scared Mickey and has stayed in his memory ever since.

If not his Guardian Angel – then what else could it possibly be?

The thought sends chills through Mickey.

He believes in Guardian Angels and remembers being told as a new entrant at school, to always leave a space on your chair to allow room for your Guardian Angel to sit next to you.

A habit he has and carries with him to this day.

Mickey drives a white 2015 Mustang which he purchased as a retirement gift to himself after paying off his mortgage. He is an authority on all music genres from the nineteen twenties through to and including the nineteen eighties and nineties.

After that, music changed for Mickey who wasn't in the least interested in soul and rap music.

He loves the rock n roll era of the 1960s but also has a strong appreciation for jazz.

Mickey is against raising the retirement age and has a strong dislike for cyclists hogging roads and riding in groups of four abreast.

In his opinion, these shining black Lycra-wearing cyclists are no better than roaches infesting our roads.

In Mickey's experience, these cyclists usually ride all over the place drifting in and out occupying lanes while chatting and ignoring motorists who are patiently following slowly behind.

On more than one occasion, after Mickey had tooted a group while trying to carefully navigate past these inconsiderate cyclists when riding more than three or four abreast while on his way to the office at six-forty-five in the morning, these road roaches surrounded his car when stopped at traffic lights and began spitting.

Like the unwanted droppings from seagulls, they left the white Mustang awash with spit and phlegm before riding off again after finishing their unwanted business.

These unwanted pests certainly lived up to their name-sake identity.

And what could he do about that?

Absolutely nothing except to call up talk-back radio and that is his beef!

There was nothing else he could do being outnumbered as he was.

These inconsiderate Lycra-wearing road hoggers cannot be reported and can ride freely on the roads without having to pay any road user charges or registration fees.

They ride without any consequence for law-breaking and Mickey has even witnessed them all going through red lights as a group together knowing there is safety in their own numbers.

Calling them out publicly is the best and only way Mickey knows to vent his built-up anger and frustration close enough to naming and shaming this scum of the roads.

He is also anti-royalist and a staunch Republican.

He voices his objection to still having the Royal family and thinks it is now time to drop the monarchy altogether and save taxpayer money.

His father Jack was from Eire who passed down stories of the Irish struggles and troubles for his family to never forget.

Mickey has strong Christian values and is a strong supporter of the preservation of life, is anti-abortion and anti-end of life.

The villa on Moonshine Valley Road is one of the original dwellings from the nineteen-twenties period.

It was love at first sight when Mickey first laid eyes on the property nestled amongst the trees and native bush.

The house is a sanctuary for Mickey hidden away out of view from people and passersby.

It reminds him of the camp he used to attend as a cub and Boy Scout.

The camp was off the main road and could only be accessed with a one-kilometre-long old dirt track drive, hidden like a jewel amongst native trees and bush.

The property was donated to the Catholic Church and used as a Christian Youth Camp from the late 1950s' and into the 1960s.

Two houses were also hidden in the dense bush above the camp and appeared empty with no one ever seeing movement from anyone entering or leaving.

Despite the apparent seclusion, there would be light blue smoke occasionally rising from the two chimneys with a light shining from within.

The houses looked eerily spooky and there was an urban myth at the time that witches occupied the houses.

Fodder for the rich and fertile minds and imagination of young children.

Witches concocting their evil spells and looking for naughty children to take away from their mummy and daddies.

There was even a stream running through the camp above which a thick rope dangled from a tree on which campers used to swing and plunge themselves off into the water.

This is always a welcome source for adventure.

When Mickey first took possession of the property, he Christened it with a bottle of bubbly and named it his own Knocknagree.

His Mustang remains off site securely garaged a small distance away at another residence which Mickey rents from an elderly widow for $75 a week – money she used and put towards gifts for her grandchildren's birthdays and Christmases.

The villa's interior is imaginatively themed to meet Mickey's creative lifestyle, memory, and interests.

The music room is in fact two rooms, warehousing fifteen thousand or so records, cassettes, and compact discs – wall to wall and floor to ceiling.

There are hundreds of 78 records preserved in their paper dust jackets, thousands of long-playing (LP) records, single 45s also in dust jackets, EP's (Extended Play) and cassette tapes.

Mickey had also purchased two restored HMV Gramophone Players as well as an array of hi-fidelity record players from the 1960s and tape recorders that were more popular in their day.

He keeps several copies of various highly collectable records and has his own Discogs Account to sell to collectors.

Mickey regularly stock takes and catalogues every item mostly for his own satisfaction but also for insurance purposes.

He has a jazz room that's arc deco designed and each of the three remaining, what would be double bedrooms, Mickey has re-created into time-period rooms – 50-60's, 60'70's and 80-90's.

He periodically redecorates and refurbishes these rooms to maintain their freshness and newness.

Nothing looks worse than faded colours, old pictures and stale-looking furnishings.

The rooms are furnished appropriately for the times and decorated accordingly with wall posters and light fittings. The light fittings are also replaced periodically.

There are beds and bookcases in each room filled with long-forgotten stories and picture books.

There are also carefully hidden speakers connected to Bluetooth devices with preselected playlists for each of the decade years.

This has become Mickey's very own time warp machine where he can escape and go back to the period of his past resurrecting it back to life with just a couple of clicks.

Away from Moonshine Valley Road and back into another time of his life, Mickey can be transported there.

Mickey's radio then bleats out a song bite, 'Well I've never been to Spain'.

And then.

"And I'm your host Tim Markham, Timothy for short—chuckles—and today we're talking about travel, destinations, unusual destinations and places you've dreamed about and discovered and places you're still waiting to discover, places still on your bucket list."

Timothy has a dinosaur of knowledge, sharing long-forgotten history and is an authority on musical genres who also hosts a nostalgia programme every Sunday where people call in to reminisce.

He also sports a tied-back greying ponytail and is eloquently spoken with a velvet voice.

"Let me know, surprise me. What are some of the mysteries you've uncovered while travelling to that special place? Come on, give us a call, and share your experiences."

"Alan wants to go to the Moon; Jesica wants to spend some time at the space station speaking of which, did you know, that is where there is a real time travel."

"Yes, in case you weren't aware, for people who orbit above the planet, time goes slower for them than on Earth which means that time on Earth is in the future when they return – fascinating stuff."

"So, Mickey, you're partially correct future time travel is possible but going back in time, well that's a different matter altogether unless you have invented a supersonic time machine or have discovered adjacent wormholes."

"Yes Barbara," as another contributor calls to join the show.

"I've already got my ticket to the Moon, Tim. Yes, well in 1969 Pan Am had a promotion and I queued up for a ticket to the moon after the year 2000."

"Marvelous," responded Tim. "Do you still have the ticket?" He continued.

"Yes, but it's only a memento now though, unless Virgin makes it more affordable though sadly, I don't think that will ever be in my lifetime," Barbara concluded her call.

"And also, Pan Am are well gone now."

The washing machine whirred away in the background now, drowning out the radio as Mickey continued with his chores.

It is Friday and Mickey always considered Friday to be the first day of the weekend.

Even before retiring as a statistical research engineer and flight planner, Mickey always called Friday his first day of the weekend to the delight of all his colleagues who cheerfully agreed, that it is always a good positive concept.

Mickey was never the one to waste time and is disciplined and organised with a to-do list for all household chores.

The To-Do List is checked off systematically with each task completed and Mickey prides himself after completing every item.

He also applies the same disciplined system for maintaining a budget and paying monthly bills on time.

So far this morning he is scheduled for an on-time arrival, a term he carried over from his operational airline days.

Penny Absalom is scheduled to visit Mickey at 1300 hours, and it is still only 1100 hours.

Penny is recently widowed after 27 years of marriage and had previously worked as a trainer also with the same airline from where she first became acquainted with Mickey.

They share common interests in music and literature, both liking Wordsworth, Keats, and Coleridge with Mickey being a fan of The Rime of the Ancient Mariner. Penny's favourite was The Presence of Love, by Samuel Taylor Coleridge.

Both also admire Oscar Wilde's stories and poetry and in particular, 'The Importance of Being Earnest.'

Mickey and Penny also share the same birthday albeit, with three years separating them, Mickey being her senior.

When Penny left to raise her children, they continued to keep in touch and would catch up annually for their birthdays.

They were close friends at work, sharing meals and break times and were often considered a unit.

However, Penny was already in a relationship with Tom and although they were both very similar, they just considered themselves as being siblings rather than friends.

Mickey always considered the term friends, as being meaningless.

A friend is someone with whom there is never an opportunity for something deeper or more romantic.

Mickey felt there was always some chemistry between them, but the time and opportunity had never presented itself in the past. He had always been open to the opportunity but kept a respectful distance while Penny and Tom were busy with their courtship and later, family life.

Both had now grown through the pressures of experiencing life and have emerged with greater wisdom, understanding and overall maturity.

Sibling is only defined as bother sister but now in this new age why not include partner and lover?

After all, it's now an age where one can decide and define one's own identity.

For someone dressing as transgender fashioning a multi-coloured ponytail, may prefer to be identified as 'my-little-pony' rather than being male or female.

"Now there's a thought," Mickey considered with a smile crossing his face and with that the image of how Penny may now be looking.

He had last seen Penny at Tom's funeral two years before dressed in black and still looking stunning.

Mickey too had looked after his health and appearance, keeping relatively trim and dressing in smart to well-dressed attire.

His hair was thinning and receding, but the greying helped him to look ever more distinguished in his sixty-nine years with a lightly trimmed silver beard.

Mickey also sported an admiral's cap on weekends and became quite the man in uniform for anyone who might be interested in uniformed men.

It just so happens that Penny does hold a secret fascination for a man in uniform and so Mickey ensures that his cap is always sitting on the right angle with every hair in place.

As the knock was delivered, Mickey felt an anxious nervousness pass over him in anticipation of opening the door.

There to greet him was someone dressed as colourfully and as beautifully as the spring day that was blooming into life.

"Penny is someone who still manages to look even better the older she becomes," Mickey thought as he gave her the once-over.

At a somewhat awkward millisecond, the words for his greeting failed him with his eyes darting over her beauty then with Penny coming to the rescue greeting, "Mickey, so lovely to finally see you again after what seems like an eternity!"

And the two embraced for a moment, probably longer than what should have been.

"Happy birthday," they both exclaimed at the same time.

"A big year and milestone for you Mickey," as she embraced him.

"Yes, seventy!"

"And you're only a few more years behind me," he responded.

They had planned to share a special lunch to celebrate the day and Penny had stopped at the local bakery to pick up sandwiches and cream buns along the way.

There was also a lemon-iced birthday cake in a box that she had pre-ordered.

She remembered that Mickey loves lemon cake, his much-preferred cake over chocolate any day.

Chocolate always seems to taste too rich.

Penny followed Mickey into the kitchen to help prepare lunch.

Mickey had already prepared the bubbles on ice waiting for their celebration.

"Oh Mickey, you've made this so wonderful," commenting on the layout of the house and themed rooms. "This is fantastic it's so unique just like you!" She marvelled. "This is really you."

"I've made it mine," he announced proudly puffing out his chest.

"You mean not to share with anyone else?" she teased.

"No, I didn't mean that. I would be happy to share this with someone special and for someone to also make their own mark and influence into this house. I just mean I've created...,"

"Don't explain," she stopped him mid-sentence, "I understand giggling."

Penny's expression suddenly changed to become blank, staring out towards, through and passed Mickey into nowhere.

Seconds like minutes passed.

"Penny!" called Mickey, "Are you Ok, what's wrong?"

"Oh sorry, Mickey, just a little bit of de 'ja' vu. The strangest thing, I have this feeling of having already been in this moment in the same conversation – that's so weird," and shakes her head before re-entering the current time zone with Mickey.

"All Good, I've experienced those types of moments myself – it certainly makes you wonder if there's anything in it, I mean having somehow been to wherever in the past or future and having the briefest of a memory with déjà vu," responded Mickey. "I think about that sort of stuff all the time."

"When I first went to Sydney, I arrived home early from work one Saturday and as I was climbing the stairs to my room. I felt very odd in the same way."

"It was weird because I had never been to Sydney before and yet I felt a déjà vu," he shared.

"Well, I was looking towards your music room, and I swear that I've seen it before, it looks so familiar it's like I've already been there like I recognised it from another time," Penny explained.

"Well, of course, you have been there haven't you – the seventies?"

"It looked like you were ready to faint," said Mickey.

"You know, there's also a theory that it may have something to do with destiny, you know, a message signalling that someone's on the right path leading to where they should be or somewhere where they are meant to belong in life," Mickey added.

Whatever it was, the moment soon passed and the two chatted over a lazy lunch with bubbles and a shandy for Penny sharing sandwiches shooting the breeze.

Tom's sudden passing was still taking its toll on Penny who still hadn't quite ended her grieving phase and Mickey provided a good shoulder to cry on and is a good listener with plenty of reassuring confidence.

Penny's social life had also come to a halt with the unexpected passing of Tom two years earlier so now Mickey's recent invitation to visit was well-timed and welcomed.

He is the enthusiastic type who has the knack for always bringing people along with him, a strong influencer.

The two reconnected throughout the afternoon and exchanged meaningful compliments with each other.

They reminisced about the time when they first met and began working together and shared their sadness for the loss of their youth and the years that have now passed by.

How quickly time seems to have disappeared from the time when starting a family.

Mickey already has two adult children, one of each. Both now have flown the coup.

This time the catch-up celebration would be a fleeting visit as Penny needed to complete some chores before leaving to pick up her eldest, Joseph, from uni.

Penny decorated the cake with a 70 candle and allowed Mickey to blow it out while making his special birthday wish.

"It's my secret," Mickey blurted and then followed by, "I wish always for more time."

"Must do this again and sooner rather than later," Mickey cried out to Penny as she clicked the safety belt.

"Call me—Friday is always a good day," Penny responded enthusiastically before driving off.

Like long-lost friends rekindling their connection and feeling the excitement and satisfaction that re-bonding brings with it, the pair separated until the next time.

As Mickey wandered back inside, he felt an overwhelming sense of absolution washing over him for all his past misgivings, mistakes, and failings.

He carried the guilt of his past relationships failing and would continuously beat himself up thinking about what more he may have done differently and how he should have been the bigger person, showing forgiveness and compassion and being a better person throughout his marriage, strained from mental illness and depression.

And then jumping straight back into another relationship blaming his divorce for being in a loveless marriage, not his fault, of course. Then that too failed.

Now, this afternoon, he felt revigorated, fresh, and clean, born again, and absolved. He felt a new life entering him with new beginnings about to start and was hopeful for what the future would bring.

Chapter Two

The music room was begging for him to enter – calling him in and his buoyant mood was equally encouraging.

Without any hesitation, Mickey entered the room and headed straight towards one of the gramophones winding it up to begin playing, Mitch Millers, 'Happy Days' and then followed by 'Yes Sir That's My Baby', two of Mickey's favourite 78 records.

Avoid any inhibitions, Mickey delighted in his mood and began dancing, round and around, arms flailing and joining triumphantly in the refrain, "Happy days are here again the skies above are clear again, let us sing a song of cheer again, happy days are here again."

And then, "Yes sir that's my baby, no sir I don't mean maybe, yes sir that's my baby now," while continuing to dance around and around.

Mickey thought back to the days when he and his mother wound up the gramophone and played all the 78's, on rainy days when he was unable to play outside.

Mickey knew all the words and would sing along with his mum.

The feeling from those times was now starting to return. From one 78 to the next, Mickey continued to play and reminisce.

"Tra la la, tweedle dee dee dee it gives me a thrill, to wake up in the morning to the Mockingbird's trill."

The music had now stopped. It had continued for some time with Mickey selecting various playlists of Jazz, Rockabilly and Fifties genres and after that, some reel-to-reel tape recordings from early morning breakfast shows of the sixties that Mickey had acquired from an old friend who used to work in radio.

The sudden silence began stirring Mickey from his slumber. It had been a jubilant and energetic time and Mickey was unaware of how much time had lapsed. He was even unaware of ever having gone to sleep.

He couldn't remember feeling tired and the last thing he heard was the time check, "Ten minutes to eight boys and girls – the school bus, is on its way don't be late," from a historic breakfast show clip from the sixties the family would listen to.

His mother, busy corralling the kids with their school bags and lunches, hurrying them on their way out the door.

The friendly announcer reached out to the kids every morning at the same time, but it was more intended to support the mums during the hectic morning run-around preparing breakfasts and lunches.

It was still daylight when Mickey finally rose from the Laz-Boy recliner and after checking the time, was surprised to discover that it was only just past four-thirty, only an hour and a half since farewelling Penny.

That hardly seemed possible.

Mickey felt as though he had been sleeping an entire night and now it seemed as though time had been suspended. He felt happy, however, that he hadn't slept for too long and that the weekend was still in front of him, waiting.

By the time Mickey had freshened and cleaned up the leftovers from lunch, it was still only six-thirty. He needed to get out and decided to leave the house for an evening stroll up to the local pub, a twenty-minute walk away.

He never drank alone, instead, he would be happy enough with a ginger bear and some company if there also happened to be any stray drinkers around.

As soon as he stepped foot outside the light changed. The warm afternoon sun became cooler with the light fading to dusk, yet it was still not yet 7 pm.

Mickey was still feeling a little muddle-headed and weird and this only confused him more.

Each step felt awkward and unsure, and Mickey was unable to shake whatever feeling had suddenly come over him.

He kept moving. The peaceful and buoyant feeling from earlier in the day had also faded and with it, his confidence.

Mickey felt troubled. Then, as his steps became more synchronised, something peculiar happened. He felt the ground beneath his feet begin to move, yet there was no sudden jolt or jerking.

It felt as though the ground was shifting more like a sliding sensation. It reminded him of the time he had visited a revolving restaurant that caused him to feel unsteady on his feet and a little bit light-headed and giddy.

As Mickey hastened, so too, did the sensation. It wasn't letting up. In fact, Mickey felt as though whatever it was, was now snapping at his heels, getting closer, chasing him.

Mickey felt panicked, too afraid to stop and was now in a jog. He needed to slow down but dared not.

Keeping up his pace, Mickey gingerly turned to look behind. While there was still light in front, behind was totally black.

Pitch darkness!

He peered towards the ground only to discover everything had disappeared.

There was nothing left. There was no road, no footpath, no greenery or side verges.

Even the shadows failed to exist. Instead, there was just emptiness.

All that Mickey had paced before was now gone – all behind him had disappeared.

Bewildered, Mickey collapsed. Surprisingly, he was still on solid ground with an air of stillness surrounding him. Nothing moved and there was no sound.

The previous sensation Mickey experienced with the ground moving had also stopped. After allowing time to regroup his emotions, Mickey felt safe enough to explore his surroundings.

He reached behind. The emptiness had now become solid again, and Mickey was now able to move his arms across the surface behind him.

The picture in front of him was now almost completely dark. Outlines were now unrecognisable with new shapes emerging.

For the first time, Mickey finally had the nerve and energy to cry out for help and he did. "Help!"

No one responded. Mickey turned his body around to where he had just come. The shapes he had left behind were also unrecognisable.

Mickey had no idea of where he had come from or where in fact he was at this very moment in time.

On hands and knees, he began clawing back the path from which he had come. The ground felt rough and unsealed, stoney with loose metal.

He clawed a short distance enough to allow him the confidence to stand and walk to continue his reclaim.

One cautious step after another slow and cautious step.

He heard a crackle of what sounded like it could be coming from a radio but was unable to determine its proximity. There were no voices, just the whirring of a radio searching for a connection to a radio signal and station.

"Hey!" He called out again. "I need help, can anyone hear me – hello!"

But still nothing, just the faint echo of his cries for help.

The radio crackling had stopped, and Mickey lit a flame from his lighter to check his watch.

Eight-fifty-seven.

But it certainly was not evening any more.

There was now daylight, but Mickey still hadn't noticed the object sitting straight in front of him.

"Hey! Watch out!" He first heard the wince and then the voice of a young girl, a voice of annoyance bordering close to sounding like she was about to lose her temper.

"Oh, I'm so terribly sorry, wasn't watching where I was going," Mickey apologised.

The startled girl looked back at him.

"I hope I haven't hurt you, are you alright?" Mickey enquired.

"I'm OK," the girl replied.

"What are you doing? Who are you?" she asked in quick succession.

"Oh, my name is Mickey, and you are?" Mickey offered his hand to the girl.

"My name is Bernice, but I hate that name. Everyone calls me Bunny because of my pet rabbit, it normally follows me around everywhere, but today my sister is looking after him," she replied.

"We're both tomboys preferring the rough and tumble more than the sweet effeminate type of girl. We much prefer the outdoors and wearing shorts and jeans rather than skirts and dresses," continued Bunny.

Bunny explained that she is a twin and her sister's name is Diane.

Mickey also shared about having a twin sister Mary.

Being a twin meant that they shared similar experiences about feeling close to the other twin and where they could somehow feel and sense situations the other twin may also be experiencing.

And Bunny was able to relate to understanding some of Mickey's experiences that he shared in conversation.

"So what do you do?" she asked, "Are you still working?"

"Well, I've recently retired and am taking it easy now. I've got lots to keep me occupied," replied Mickey.

"What about you?"

"Are you still at school?"

"This is my last year, today I'm on study leave."

"I only have another few months and then it's out of school for good," she exclaimed punching the air.

"I'm not sure what I will do when I leave, my parents want me to work for the gazette, you know the local rag. But I hate writing. I even hate writing essays," Bunny continued.

Bunny was wearing earplugs and listening to a transistor radio.

"What are you doing, are you from around here?" Bunny asked.

"I'm not sure," replied Mickey "I'm hoping you can help me; I think I'm lost."

"I don't recognise this place, where is this? What's the name of this place?"

"This is Riverstone of course," Bunny replied.

"Oh, and can you tell me what day it is – the date, please?"

"Oh come on. What's wrong with you, it's Saturday, April 16, 1966, of course."

"Are you alright old man? Do you need help?"

"Did you say 1966?" Mickey had a confused look on his face.

"I should be twelve years old," he thought.

"Are you sure?" He questioned Bunny. "Sure, that it's Saturday 16 April 1966?"

"Of course, why wouldn't I be?"

"It's my birthday," he said without a lot of certainty.

"Today? Well, Happy Birthday, old man… how old are you? Sorry, I shouldn't have asked."

"It's OK, in reality, I'm much closer to seventy than twenty," Mickey responded.

"What do you mean, in reality?" questioned Bunny.

"Are you sure of the year, 1966?"

"Well, what else would it be?"

"I'm not sure anymore," said the old man. Mickey was certainly beginning to feel his real age and looked back at Bunny.

"What are you listening to?"

"Wild Thing, la da da da da da, you make my heart sing," Bunny demonstrated moving her head and arms in a dancing motion.

"It's the most unusual and weirdest song of 1966!" she proclaimed continuing to hum along.

"Yes, I know it," agreed Mickey, "I remember."

"You know this song?" Bunny asked surprised.

"Yes, I've heard it before," Mickey replied. "And I agree, it is weird."

"But I still like it," Bunny continued. "It's real groovy."

"So, are you from around here?" Bunny asked again.

"I'm from Riverstone, living on Moonshine Valley Road," replied Mickey.

"Yes, well this is Valley Road Riverstone, but I haven't heard of a Moonshine Valley Road or whatever it is," replied Bunny.

"Anyway, is there anything I can do to help you or anyone you know who is able to come and help you – I can try and contact them for you?" Bunny checked with a caring and sincere tone in her voice.

"No, I'll be OK, thanks all the same."

"Well, Happy Birthday again old man, hope you enjoy your day and have a good one," as she up and left with her transistor radio and repositioned the earplugs in her ears.

She left and headed south along Valley Road.

Mickey checked his watch again – nine-seventeen.

Mickey also needed a newspaper to check the date. He never doubted that Bunny was not being truthful but like the 'Doubting Thomas', he needed to check for himself.

"And what if it is real, that it is indeed 1966, how very scary and how is that possible and what next?" All the questions crossed his mind and made his stomach churn.

Mickey checked the newsstand – the newspaper clearly showed the date printed, Saturday 16 April 1966.

"This isn't reality!"

Mickey was alone with no one he could turn to for help or share his concerns.

In 1966, Mickey was not even living in Riverstone. He was twelve years old, living four hundred miles north in the big city and still going to school.

Mickey felt that this must now be the time and or a sign for him to seize the opportunity to revisit exactly where he was in 1966.

If this is a new reality, then he wants to take advantage of the situation to rediscover what he had previously left behind a long time before.

But how would he do that? He had no money, well no legal tender for this time. Then, the currency was still pounds, shillings, and pence and not dollars and cents.

He decided to hitchhike and was lucky enough to catch a ride from a hippy shortly after sticking his thumb out.

"Hey man, jump in," as the hippy stopped alongside Mickey.

"Hey, I've got no bread man," Mickey explained jumping into the wagon.

"I lost my wallet – got nothing at all," Mickey continued.

"Oh bummer, jump in anyway, the ride's free – how much do you need? I can let go a little," the hippy offered handing over five-bob.

"Oh, much appreciated, that should help," thanked Mickey.

"Help yourself to any loose change you can find on the floor," The hippy also offered pointing to the floor and around the back seat.

And Mickey managed to pick up another couple of bob in pennies and threepences.

"Hey man, my name is Luke, are you turned on?" the hippy asked offering a reefer at the same time.

"Thanks, Luke, I'm Mike," as he accepted a toke from the reefer.

"Hey dude that's so cool, being old and turned on, you know what I mean – no offence and all, never expect old dudes to understand and get turned on," Luke acknowledged and the two shook hands briefly as Luke changed gear.

They chatted freely throughout the half-hour ride and before Mickie hopped out, Luke reached behind and scrounged a handful of more pennies from the floor of the back seat and handed these to Mickey who graciously filled his jean pockets.

"These will weigh you down," the hippie chuckled before driving off.

As Mickey was busy filling his pockets, he came across half a crown that had been wrapped in a ten-bob note.

But as he discovered this, he tried alerting Luke, but the wagon quickly sped away.

There was still an hour's wait for the bus and Mickey was now able to afford the shilling fare, pulling out twelve pennies and thereby reducing the bulge in his jean pockets.

He had now accepted and readjusted to his new time zone as he settled into the seat for the remaining journey ahead.

He still had all the time in the world to catch up on what had been happening with local and global history as he unfolded the paper. But how much would he remember?

"Farmers are expected to suffer huge financial losses caused by severe floods after losing newborn calves and lambs."

The paper reported that market gardeners have also been affected by damage to their crops, "And it remains unsure if there will be any government relief for farmers," The paper reported.

History would later show that there was financial relief.

The Beatles were still receiving dissension over Lennon's comment that being more popular than Jesus, despite having already held a press conference to clarify the context of what Lennon had said.

American fans were still trampling and burning Beatle records, books, and memorabilia in the street.

"What do the stars say?" he pondered as he turned to the horoscopes.

"Sit back and relax, this is your time, the stars are aligned, and new fortunes will not escape you. A good time for those seeking a job change."

"A marriage proposal is imminent, and romance is in the air."

"Lucky numbers, 12, 14, 6, 8 and 9."

When Mickey alighted at his city destination, he felt some lost familiarity pass over him as in déjà vu but at the same time with it not being déjà vu.

He recognised the shabby old terminus with pot-holed footpaths. He then saw and remembered some of the old bills posted on vacant buildings and walls.

"Girls! Girls! Girls! Nude-Girls!" read one bill outside the bus stop.

My mother would always turn me away or find ways to distract me from reading and looking at such bills. One of her ways was offering to buy hot chips to share as we waited for the bus.

Oh, and I could now smell them again!

The little shop was still there.

Ma's Best Chips! No, it's not, I'm here.

A carton of hot delicious chips for only sixpence filled and satisfied my hungry and rumbling tummy.

Here I am, an old man on his seventieth birthday on the streets alone. At any time, I may well be picked up as a vagrant, a derelict hobo with no fixed abode.

Who knows where it will be that I sleep tonight? It may well be a jail cell.

I wanted to conserve the remaining gains in my pockets from the ride with Luke and decided to try my hand at hitchhiking again.

And just like that, like fisherman's luck – another ride. In fact, another two rides took me almost to my hometown, Henderson.

Chapter Three

It is certainly a shameful, disgraceful, and dishonourable legacy that German, Robert Ramm, has left upon his future descendants, if any of his legacy.

Robert Ramm, commander of the German submarine, UB123 lay in wait, lurking, beneath the neutral waters of Ireland in the port of Kingston Dublin – waiting to pounce like the cowardly animal that he was bringing unforgivable and everlasting shame upon his family name.

It was the tenth hour of the tenth day of the tenth month, one month before the end of World War 1 in 1918.

Jack had only been in class a short time before hearing the explosions shortly before nine on that Thursday morning.

The first torpedo had missed its target.

The second and third torpedoes were direct hits, the second piercing the mail room on the RMS Leinster where 22 postal workers were at work crossing the Irish Sea on their way to Holyhead Wales.

Only one survived!

Over five hundred other passengers and crew were slaughtered by that infamous German, Robert Ramm on that mournful day.

A day that had devastating effects on families like ours and that would forever be unforgivably etched in the memories of so many families—forever!

Shame on all Robert Ramm descendants!

Joe mortally felt the shock wave ripping through the hull, tearing him apart, and separating his love of a promised life from his wife and family!

Joe was Gone!

"Joe is gone!" Repeated Agnes, Joe's wife inconsolably.

"Joe's gone!"

"Joe's gone!"

"Joe's gone, Oh Dear Lord!"

"Oh, Dear Lord, God Bless Us and Save Us! Oh, Dear Lord!"

Jack had lost his beloved father.

Jack, together with his five siblings had all lost their dad and now their mother, a widow.

The ship had only been four nautical miles away from the port of Kingston Dublin and en route to Holyhead, Wales.

The schoolboy's intuition told him in that instant that his life was about to change – forever.

And it did.

Just four months following his ninth birthday, Jack became the new 'man of the house' becoming the new breadwinner to support his widowed mother, himself and five siblings.

There was no government welfare then and the insurer refused to pay out on Joe's life insurance as the policy documents were inside the breast pocket of his uniform jacket.

The company declined on the basis that the widow was unable to provide any proof of her deceased husband's policy.

Agnes Elizabeth was now on her own without the crucial support she desperately needed and with no family around close to her that was able to help her and her crippled family.

Agnes had relatives living in New Zealand and made the courageous decision to immigrate with the family; Joe, Jack, Ann, Bessy, Marie, and Ronnie (Veronica).

Within the hour, Jack was removed from school never to return, ending his childhood forever.

In 1921 the family departed their home in Dublin and sailed via the Panama Canal arriving on the shores of New Zealand in April 1921.

They first moved to Gisborne before settling in Auckland.

Papers had reported an alarming news story of their ship almost sinking after a cargo of steel in the cargo hold broke loose and moved forward during rough seas crossing the Atlantic.

The ship's bow became submerged after entering a steep trough and struggled to recover and rise again over the waves.

Jack remembered the event when the ship began shuddering uncontrollably before righting itself again.

On Sunday, April 30, 1978, Jack and Margaret stood outside the front door of 10 Whitworth Place Drumcondra Dublin 9 Eire.

The door was opened by a frail elderly woman in her early nineties.

Crumbling with her tears, the old woman reached out her uncontrollable shaking hand towards Jack and Margaret.

Fifty-seven years after being ripped away from his beloved country and home, Jack had finally returned and was now in the arms of his deceased mother's sister – Aunt Martha and standing outside the same house Joe had left on that fateful last day before leaving for his job at the GPO on board the RMS Leinster, Thursday morning October 10, 1918.

Jack's childhood was ripped away from his soul in the same instant that Joe's life was ripped away while diligently working to support his family.

Jack had returned to exact his own revenge – to mercilessly hunt down that German swine, Commander Robert Ramm.

He was nevertheless spared from having to commit such a mortal sin, the hatred he had harboured for this man his entire life.

Like the fleeing Judas Robert Ramm had become, he was soon to come face to face with his own fate.

Ramm's escape route to return to Germany had become infested with mimes laid with the purpose of eliminating and destroying his sub.

Within days, Ramm had met his own demise with the German submarine being snarled up in the minefield and finally destroyed.

Martha's brother Charlie, also in his nineties, shared the same house, both brother and sister who remained single looking after one another and receiving regular weekly visits from the Church and the Holy Eucharist with blessings.

Charlie was a retired musician playing the piano and who travelled around cities entertaining with his small orchestra.

Charlie was now very much aware of his own mortality and generously donated sums of money to the Church to offer indulgences for his soul.

However, he also held a strong distrust for the Church, and particularly Saint Vincent De Paul, whom he believed were only interested in his money and property being left to the Church.

Margaret followed Jack up the stairs to the room he once shared with his siblings.

The beds were still there and remained untouched like the relics of history still clinging to the spiritual belonging of the children's souls from their last night before departing for the shores of New Zealand fifty-seven years ago.

It was still all there, even the old musty smell of the long-departed years.

Jack breathed in the musty air, holding it in his lungs and remembering the sadness that he had been brought back to revisit.

Everything else in the house was still the same the old kitchen and front room where the visitors sat enjoying copious cups of strong Irish tea regaling the past and families from the Antipodes.

Jack and Margaret made several visits to the house and Martha always stuffed a handful of notes into their pockets before leaving.

Throughout his entire life, Jack remained a troubled soul who distanced himself away from social company, preferring his own lost in the pages of books educating himself in history and geography.

Despite his lifelong difficulties, Jack never stopped supporting those around him for his entire life.

A selfless man firstly for his widowed mother and later after marrying at the late age of forty-three and raising his own three children.

He opened his wallet every Wednesday night at the dinner table handing most of his pound and ten-shilling notes over to

Margaret, his wife, to manage the household utilities and groceries.

He withheld a few notes for his pocket money to help subsidise his racing money.

He was always careful with his bets, only betting for wins and never making place bets.

He was always very firm with this principle and never budged nor could be persuaded to ever take a horse for a place bet.

As far as he was concerned, it was a wasted bet.

"It's either a win or nothing at all," He believed.

Jack studied form, the jockey, and the trainers, and even went to watch horse time trials.

He was usually successful with his weekly racing budget, collecting on a few small wins that he would add to his savings.

After growing his racing budget over a period of several weeks, Jack would then prepare for an upcoming important race meet to splurge big time on a nag he had been following and watching the performance of at trials.

So many key parties Jack depended on for racing wins and success, the trainer, the track, and the jockey as well as consistent performance.

On the day, the one horse and the one bet and on the nose.

That's all that mattered when all the elements were aligned.

Most of the time Jack would come home with pockets full, quid's ahead and brimming with a widened Irish smile.

But there were also times when the smile frowned, and everyone just knew to keep away from Dad.

Not a good time to ask for pocket money after a bad day at the races.

We kids also lost out and were forced to wait another week before collecting any allowance.

That meant no spending on snacks and treats from the school tuck shop.

But overall, Jack was smart with his money and always made sure he kept to his limits and did not chase bad money after bad as can easily happen when gambling with cards.

Jack explained that he always knew when it was time to walk away and always did.

He also tithed every week to the church without fail.

Jack worked forty hours a week commuting to and home from the city every day up until the age of seventy-two when he was forced to finally retire due to failing health.

Jack grew into a man and a devoted father any child would be proud of having as a father who died three months short of his eighty-sixth birthday.

Chapter Four

Waiting for the nine-thirty Saturday morning bus, Ivan greeted the approaching Jack, "Kako Ste," a Dalmatian greeting.

Jack, who was purposeful and determined with his stride, acknowledged the greeting with just a nod of his head and a wave of his hand.

He was a man of few words with an inherent distrust of most people and was not one for small talk or wasting words, though he always remained polite and civil with everyone.

He trusted nobody with his words, believing that it was not safe to blab and volunteer information.

People gossip and use their own words against you warning, "Oh, Snow told me that," or "Do you know what Snow was talking about?"

Snow was Jack's nickname, having white hair that he fashioned into a comb-over long before it ever became fashionable to do so.

Despite his advancing years towards retirement age, Jack maintained a trim physique and lied about his age, usually shaving a respectable ten years off his actual date of birth.

That way, records would not show any creep towards the looming and dreaded retirement age.

No one ever doubted Jack when giving his dob and always got away with what he'd said.

Jack always dressed professionally even when going to the track, with grey trousers, a navy-blue blazer, and a cravat with a cheese cutter cap.

And today Jack sat alone on the bus contemplating his mission.

He had one single objective today, one bet, one horse, and one race.

When it was over, Jack would leave the track like the assassin alone and without saying a word and keeping poker-faced without any emotion to catch the late afternoon bus and return home to his family.

He only allowed a smile after settling into his seat for the journey home.

After Sunday Mass, the family would gather around the table for the Sunday roast.

Mickey, Mary, and younger sister Frances would be entertained by Jack's natural storytelling ability from his vast array of characters and situations.

The Old Wolf, King of the Billy Goats, and Bill Sykes all lived on the North Shore and were notorious for their antics with the locals.

And there were also the Four Baldy-Headed Kidnappers who lived on Beam Rock Lighthouse.

And when each of the stories was about to end, the brood would ask, "What happened next…tell us about…and so on," until an exhausted Jack would leave his unfinished meal to complete outdoor chores.

Entertaining and original as each of the stories always were, they were delivered straight from his brain and never recorded or written down for future prosperity.

Chapter Five

Mickey was almost home, and as it was not too much further, he decided to walk the remaining distance. The landscape is semi-rural, passing lots of paddocks of lifestyle properties with grazing livestock along the way.

It was like walking home from school, this time without the bag slung across his shoulder.

The afternoon sun had cast a long shadow in front as he laboured the steep rise of the road.

The last time he walked this same path, was as a seventeen-year-old returning from school.

Then, he had a dense and full head of auburn-coloured hair that he wore proudly like a crown.

Even then he would imagine how it would look forty or fifty years' time.

Now, looking at the shadow, he saw a more rounded hunched-over man with thinning hair walking ahead of him.

The once youthful stature had long disappeared with a man struggling with each step and feeling breathless.

It saddened him to no longer see the schoolboy as it still didn't seem all that long ago he was still very much alive.

Mickey stopped beside a paddock for a spell, Thomastown ambled on over as he always did to the schoolboy offering his leftovers from an uneaten school lunch.

Horses always enjoyed chomping down and munching on the uneaten apples.

The noise sounded delicious and always made Mickey feel regretful that he hadn't chomped on the apple himself instead.

On one occasion, Mickey fed grease-proof wrappers along with uneaten sandwiches to the greedy nag that could not wait and proceeded to munch away before Mickey had the chance to open his hand.

This angered the nag so much that it retracted its ears and stomped its hooves with nostrils flaring!

This time there were no offerings but that didn't stop the retired nag from coming on over for a nosy.

He nuzzled up to Mickey and snorted giving him the once over with his cold wet nose.

"Could he still sense that familiar scent? Could he still tell it was the schoolboy standing in front of him, albeit a much older Mickey?" He wondered and hoped that he did as he caressed the horse's neck and mane.

Mickey reminded himself that as it's Saturday there will be no chance of running into his younger self returning from school to also stop at the fence.

But hey, he did wonder what would happen if that did occur.

"What would quantum physics say?"

He wouldn't have to wait long.

There, halfway up the road, stood the old grey fibro-light house with a flat roof.

And there are people outside running in and around inside and out with music playing—celebrating.

Mickey could hear "Monday, Monday," with the echoes of, "Can't trust that day."

"Just like school, I hate that day Monday," he heard someone yell.

Straight after that was The Vogues with, 'Five o'clock World'.

And there was Mickey!

Outside with his twin, Mary.

Oh, look at him. Look at that boy with his innocence with his sister.

Look! wow!

Look how young and thin he had once been and so energetic.

The woman who stepped outside with lemonade and a plate of sausage rolls was Margaret, Mickey's mother! Jack's wife!

"Look! Mum!" He thought aloud but dared not to yell out.

No one had yet seen or noticed the old man approaching the house.

"Oh Mum," he was beginning his grieving again for the sudden and unexpected death of his mother in 1982 from a heart attack.

"Oh Mum," he wanted to reach out again and hold her, and there was so much more he longed to be able to speak with her and ask her for long belated advice.

He wanted to share his own family experiences and achievements.

Oh, there is so much unfinished time that has been cruelly stolen away.

"Oh, Mum!" He was wishing and thinking, thinking of how much we all take life and people for granted, not thinking that people whom we love so dearly will not always be with us.

We are all guaranteed to not survive, but we are never fully ready for the hour when loved ones cease to belong in our lives.

We never prepare ourselves for tragedies and personal family losses.

Mother's loss was such a huge tragedy for the family.

Mickey then recalled the plaque that hung on the kitchen wall – Mothers' Burdens.

"Mothers' Burdens."

"She mourns for the children she will never have—

She mourns seeing, knowing, and hearing the things she should never have—

Searches for the lost time that she will never have again."

Mickey also grieved for the loss of his twin and wanted to reach out to hug her.

Mary also passed away from a brain tumour in 2019.

Oh, there is so much to say to everyone, so many lost loves, lives, and opportunities.

And to the friends that had left behind their innocence and childhoods and entered adulthood.

All these emotions raced through Mickey's bloodstream with his heart pumping madly, and that suddenly brought a thought that stopped him in his tracks.

His brain was now pounding!

Yes, while he had already accepted and adjusted to the time shift while travelling north in the company of others, Mickey had not thought it through enough to consider the consequences of what it would mean to come across people he knew.

To recognise people from his past, and still in the past and more importantly, to recognise his younger self from that same time!

And he did see himself – there in the distance!

The younger Mickey, the slender boy playing in a group of other kids!

Oh, how shocked he felt to know and witness this event, to see himself and to know it was real, really happening – really himself and so close to, from a different time!

"Two Me's – the same me!" he thought.

He wanted to reach out to grab that boy to hold on to that innocence that had long been lost for so many years.

Mickey was unable to move any closer out of fear – fear of the unknown, of the consequences.

No matter how he feels, this situation is real at this point in time and space, there is nothing now Mickey can do to change the situation.

He began feeling a claustrophobic panic, of feeling helplessly trapped with no possible escape, and with no one around to help.

He may as well be drifting alone in outer space, hopelessly lost in space!

Now lost in time-space!

Mickey felt unbelievably shocked, shaking his head standing and staring!

Staring back at himself and the same younger Mickey who is not yet looking or seeing him, recognising the older Mickey!

He decided to change direction to avoid the risk of clashing with past lives and turned to cut across the paddocks that belonged to his three Irish aunts; Ronnie Marie and Bess.

Their other sister Ann lived a few yards further up the road with her husband Dan who owned a general store.

Each of the aunts was already in their mid to late fifties and Ronnie, Marie, and Bess, all lived together on the lifestyle property in an old stone farmhouse.

A paddock separated them from the house where Jack and his family lived.

Each of the aunts took on various household duties to support their household.

Marie's role was to look after the household maintenance including building and repairs as well as the plumbing and electrical.

Marie is very resourceful and calls on the assistance of specialised tradesmen in the local community when needed.

Payment is usually with fresh baking and the occasional moonshine from their brother Joe's still.

The aunts maintain a strong rapport with the whole community, most of whom have their own lifestyle farms.

Marie is the tom-boy who never objects to rolling up her sleeves and taking on the tougher chores and manual work around the property and getting her hands dirty.

Each of the aunts is more than capable of performing their own household tasks including cooking, baking, sewing, knitting, washing, and ironing.

Marie is also a skilled hair stylist who is always in regular demand for sets, perms, and rinses.

Ronnie's the homemaker and mother to daughter Veronica.

Ronnie was also widowed during the Second World War by a German and struggled through her life.

Ronnie keeps house by baking and cooking delicious treats and meals.

Any leftover scraps are fed to the chooks.

Today all three are in the far end of one of the paddocks, burning off gorse. When all together, dressed in gumboots overalls and straw hats and armed with pitchforks and pick axes and spades, they became a force to contend with.

The youngest and fiercest of all three aunts is Ronnie who has a short-fused temper and who is unafraid of confronting any conflict head-on and chasing trespassers across the paddocks until they are caught and wrestling them to the ground in a tight hold around the scruff of their necks.

Ronnie is fearless.

She has a fearsome reputation among the local schoolboy delinquents.

The gorse was well alight blazing ten to twenty feet high and licking the sky.

There is a good chance that Mickey could go unnoticed crossing the far-end paddock since their backs were turned away and keeping a watchful eye on the blaze.

All very astute, but it was Ronnie who first caught a glimpse of Mickie out from the corner of her eye.

No need to rub her eyes to double-check.

Ronnie was certain and gave chase after the trespasser.

"Hey, stop where you are! This is private property! Get off our land!" came her fierce like and threatening war cry.

Ronnie had already got up speed with her chase before she had even finished shouting and using cursing cusses with colourful Gaelic blasphemies.

Ronnie had the speed Mickie no longer had, and try as he did, she was gaining on him.

He had to keep going panting with every stride.

Out of breath, Mickey was beginning to slow with Ronnie gaining on his heels.

The rickety fence was in sight for his escape but as he prepared to sidle his way across by holding down the barbed wire, Mickey lost control and collapsed feeling the full force of what felt like an All-Black's rugby tackle.

Her words came back to haunt him as he lay defenceless and cowling from fear after feeling his ear being brutely twisted hard.

"You're not to play in the paddocks! I don't know how many times I've already told your mother and father!" And felt his ear being so severely twisted to force him to his knees.

He had been dropped from behind the knees and was now facing the dirt smelling the stale dried cow dung in his face.

His captor was Ronnie, who gasped after seeing him.

"Jack!" she exclaimed.

"Is that you Jack?" she continued in her Irish brogue.

"Jack?"

I'm not Jack but Mickey did know and understand exactly who Ronnie was talking about.

"Jack's my father." Mickey realised.

Jack was already an old man when Mary, Mickey and Frances were born.

He married Margaret when he was fifty and was now in his early seventies.

As Micky had aged, he began to take on more of his father's features, looking more and more like him.

"Today I am seventy." Mickey acknowledged.

"Today he realised, I am him."

"I've become my father!"

"Jack, what are you doing running like this?"

I had no choice but to play along.

"I didn't want to disturb you while you were busy with the gorse; I was on my way to the village." Mickey tried explaining.

Everyone called the local township the village.

"Are you all right Jack?" Ronnie asked.

"Yes, I'll be OK," Mickey responded in a somewhat morbid depressive tone.

"What's wrong?"

"Did my dough in at the track," I thought a good time for a little white lie to cover for my loss of funds.

"Where? Avondale or the TAB?" integrated Ronnie.

The whole family were racing mad including Jack and all his siblings. They could talk about racing day and night.

Each was the expert who was able to speak with authority and knowledge though none had become rich from any substantial winnings.

The one radio station was always tuned in for racetrack broadcast meets around the country.

"And as they have all lined up, now in position, and they're racing this time," was the starting cry before the commentator continued to report on the early race leads and positions as they headed around the track.

Our national sports events then were rugby, racing, and beer.

"Avondale," I embellished.

"Can't remember too much as I had a bit of a moment, I was going to the window and then don't know much about what happened after that," I lied before saying I had lost a couple of quid, almost a man's wages for a week in 1966.

Mickey had no knowledge of any racehorse names, so his sudden loss of memory was a plausible excuse.

"You got to start looking after yourself now – you're not getting any younger and you're not a young man anymore." Ronnie reminded me.

"I say, you're not a young man anymore," Ronnie had the habit of repeating herself to herself when walking away and ending with a laughing cackle as if to say, "I know, I know what I'm talking about. As I say, I'm right you know."

"Go and let yourself in at the house, Marie will be down shortly to fix lunch."

So, Mickie took up the offer after picking himself up and dusting himself down.

"You're not a young man," Marie reiterated as she made her entrance after moving the cats that had encircled her feet and removing her gumboots.

"You should go and see Reg," our local GP who lived closer to the city, Marie went on.

"Go and see Reg," she repeated as she put the kettle on the coal burner.

Mickey felt at home again sitting in familiar surroundings and speaking with his long-deceased aunts.

Marie brewed a strong hot cup of tea and brought over a freshly baked scone Ronnie had made earlier that morning before leaving for the paddocks.

"I need a couple of quid," Mickey blurted out.

"Well, I can't afford to give you a couple of quid," retorted Marie and just then, Bessie also walked in ready for lunch, Ronnie remained outside keeping a careful watch on the fire that was now reduced to a much smaller flame and smoulder.

"I can give you ten bob Jack, but no more," Marie offered as she wandered off to her room. "And you'll have to pay me back once you get paid mind you."

"How much are you looking for?" the kinder Bessie offered.

"Will ten bob be OK?"

"Oh, thank you, that will certainly help," Mickey acknowledged as the two aunts returned with their offerings.

"Thank you both."

"But please, don't say anything to Margaret, she'll kill me if she finds out," Margaret being my mother.

Mickey had accumulated almost two quid which will be more than enough to help see him through.

The silver in his jeans was weighing him down and jingled as he moved.

Unsure of his next move, Mickey was certain that he must leave but for where?

He dares not return to the house he grew up in just a little further down the road and separated by one of the paddocks.

He thought about Knocknagree which had dorms and ablutions but that was some distance away, at least a good three to four miles and he would need to hike through the cemetery.

He had a vague idea of where Knocknagree was located but finding the off-road winding track may prove challenging particularly if there is no signage.

But having to cross the cemetery this late in the day is something that didn't inspire Mickey.

If he is somehow lucky with finding Knocknagree, he hoped that it would not be in use or occupied by any of Baden-Powel's mob.

The geese had all been fed but the cats and dogs were all congregating again around the front porch waiting for their titbits – always on the scrounge for any food scraps.

And then there is me, Mickey, preparing to exit the front porch when to my astonishment Margaret appears, walking down the stony path.

"Quick please," I pleaded, "I'm not here—Margaret's coming!" as I dashed back into the house to hide in the bathroom.

"Please don't say that I'm here or that you've seen me," I continued.

Everyone began to panic as I barged my way through to the bathroom.

"Go outside," one of them screamed.

But it was too late.

There was even more commotion as Margaret made her entrance through the din and chorus of barking yelping and snapping dogs at her feet.

All three in unison with their Irish brogue, welcomed the visitor while at the same time shooing away all the critters with unsympathetic tones.

"Come in, come in," they all welcomed and insisted.

"I've just stopped by to drop the lamb joint off to you while passing." Margaret offered.

"You haven't seen Jack, have you? – he should be coming by on the bus from Avondale soon."

"No," as they all shook their heads.

"Oh quick, I need to use the toilet," Mother squirmed as she started to head straight towards where I was hiding.

He heard the hurried footsteps and then a saving voice, "Use the outside lavie, I think someone's already using it."

But too late!

Mother and I finally came face to face and eyeball to eyeball after not seeing each other for so many years.

"Who, who are you?" Margaret asked looking dismayed and puzzled.

And before I had the time to respond.

"No! You're not Jack!"

"Who are you?"

And then!

"Mother!" I exclaimed feeling heart warmed and pleased that she was now with me again, standing in front of me – after all this time.

"Mum! Behold your son Mickey!" and as I spoke, the heavens opened, and lightning flashed as thunder rolled across the sky and cracked.

My mother was gone and now, so was I.

"It's what gets me up in the morning, it's what gets me out of bed," the radio bleated.

"It's what gets me to the next room, out of here and into the next dimension," it continued.

"Time, yes listeners, time."

"In the early hours of the morning, I want to talk about time, what it means to you – how do you manage your time and what is the mystery of time?"

"Have you ever been there, have you ever been out of time and if so, where?"

"What are some of your experiences – share them with us."

"My name is Mickey and I'm your host during this late night and right through into the early morning hours of the new day."

It was now twenty-three hundred hours on Wednesday 17 October 2018.

"In a few hours it will be the one-hundred-year anniversary of the sinking of the RMS Leinster," Mickey was thinking.

He should be there with the rest of the family, on the ferry in Dun Laoghaire to throw a wreath down to Joe.

He was very regretful that he couldn't make the long journey due to health reasons.

"Good morning, Penny."

"I would like to talk about déjà vu," Penny continued.

"I'm always experiencing them, and I don't know what it means."

"Oh wow! That's weird," it's just happened to me Mickey laughed and said, "Just kidding, carry on Penny."

After a few more late-night callers and intermittent ad breaks, "Now thinking and talking about time, who can remember this?"

"Wild Thing,
You make my heart sing,
You make everything groovy,
Wild Thing
Wild Thing
I think I love you
But I wanna know for sure,
So come on hold me tight,

I love you," as the song played.

Mickey's twelfth birthday will always be a memorable day for him.

For Mickey and Mary, it remained a popular table topic for them to regale years later.

After returning home from his day at the races, Jack was unable to remove his ear-to-ear grin.

It was the day of his big win.

'Heavens Above' had romped home and paid a handsome dividend with Jack collecting one hundred and forty-seven pounds.

While excitedly sharing his tale, Jack pulls out a whooping wad of notes from his wallet and slips five pounds to each of the three children.

Half of the remaining wad went to Margaret with Jack proudly pocketing the rest.

It was the first time he ever had so much in his bulging wallet.

A card slipped under the door waiting for Mickie to open and read.

"Happy Birthday Old Man,
Enjoy Your Special Day,
Love Always,
Bunny XXX."

The End

John Samuel Robinson ©